BEHIND THE MASK

YANGSOOK CHOI

FRANCES FOSTER BOOKS
Farrar, Straus and Giroux
New York

Copyright © 2006 by Yangsook Choi
All rights reserved
Distributed in Canada by Douglas & McIntyre Ltd.
Color separations by Embassy Graphics
Printed and bound in the United States of America by Phoenix
Color Corporation
Designed by Barbara Grzeslo
First edition, 2006
10 9 8 7 6 5 4 3 2 1

www.fsgkidsbooks.com

Library of Congress Cataloging-in-Publication Data
Choi, Yangsook.
    Behind the mask / Yangsook Choi.— 1st ed.
      p. cm.
    Summary: Kimin, a young Korean-American boy, has trouble
deciding on a Halloween costume, but as he looks through an old
trunk of his grandfather's things, he suddenly unlocks a childhood
mystery.
    ISBN-13: 978-0-374-30522-2
    ISBN-10: 0-374-30522-6
    [1. Halloween—Fiction. 2. Masks—Fiction. 3. Grandfathers—
Fiction. 4. Korean Americans—Fiction.] I. Title.

PZ7.C446263Beh 2006
[E]—dc22
                                              2005045950

To Yoonseo and Jion

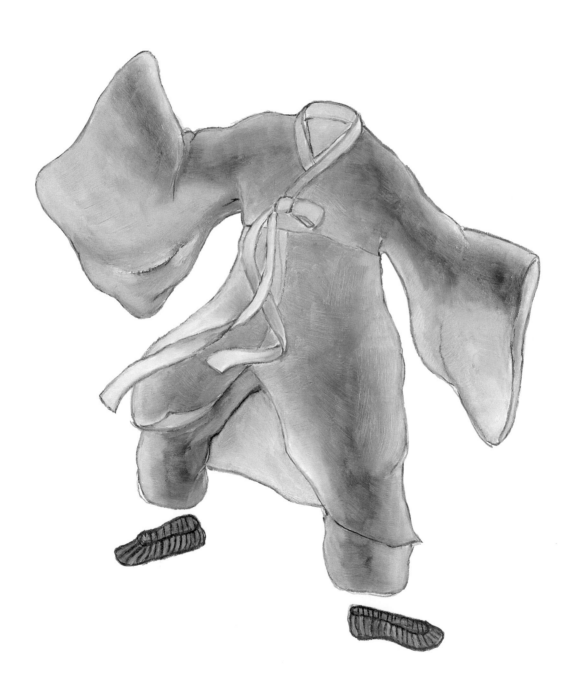

Kimin looked out the window into the wide night sky. In two days it would be Halloween, and the glowing pumpkin on his windowsill would light the way for all the wandering spirits.

But he still hadn't decided what he wanted to be this Halloween. His mother had said he might find some interesting things for a costume among his grandfather's belongings, but Kimin wasn't so sure about that.

Kimin's mother brought two boxes up from the basement.
"I'll leave these in your room so you can look through them in the
morning," she said. "And do be careful," she added. "Some of
Grandfather's things are valuable. They're family treasures."

Kimin knew that his grandfather had been a famous dancer
in Korea. Still, he wished his mother hadn't left the boxes in his
room.

Kimin got into bed and pulled the blanket over his head so he wouldn't have to look at Grandfather's boxes. He wondered why they made him so uncomfortable, and then he remembered something he thought he had buried . . .

It was a memory of the last time he had seen his grandfather, in Korea.

Grandfather was old and didn't always recognize Kimin. Sometimes he called him by his uncle's name. But Kimin didn't mind. He liked to sit and talk with him—Kimin speaking English, Grandfather answering in Korean. But mostly Grandfather just smiled at him, and that made Kimin feel good until one night when he couldn't sleep . . .

A light shone from Grandfather's room. Kimin got up and peeked through a hole in the rice-paper door. Grandfather sat on the floor with his back to Kimin. He was bent over a box. Kimin was happy to see that his grandfather was awake, too, and opened the door. Grandfather turned around. But he looked gruesome!

Kimin was terrified and never told anyone about that night. After that he didn't want to be alone with his grandfather. And now Grandfather was dead.

In the bright light of morning, Grandfather's boxes didn't seem so menacing. "I will only look at the pictures," Kimin told himself as he opened the smaller box labeled *Grandfather's photos*.

The top layer was mostly pictures of Kimin and Grandfather—Kimin as a baby in his grandfather's arms, Kimin as a toddler in a park with Grandfather, and Kimin with aunts and uncles and cousins he hardly knew. But then there were pictures Kimin had never seen, of dancers wearing face masks performing before a crowd. Were these pictures of his grandfather?

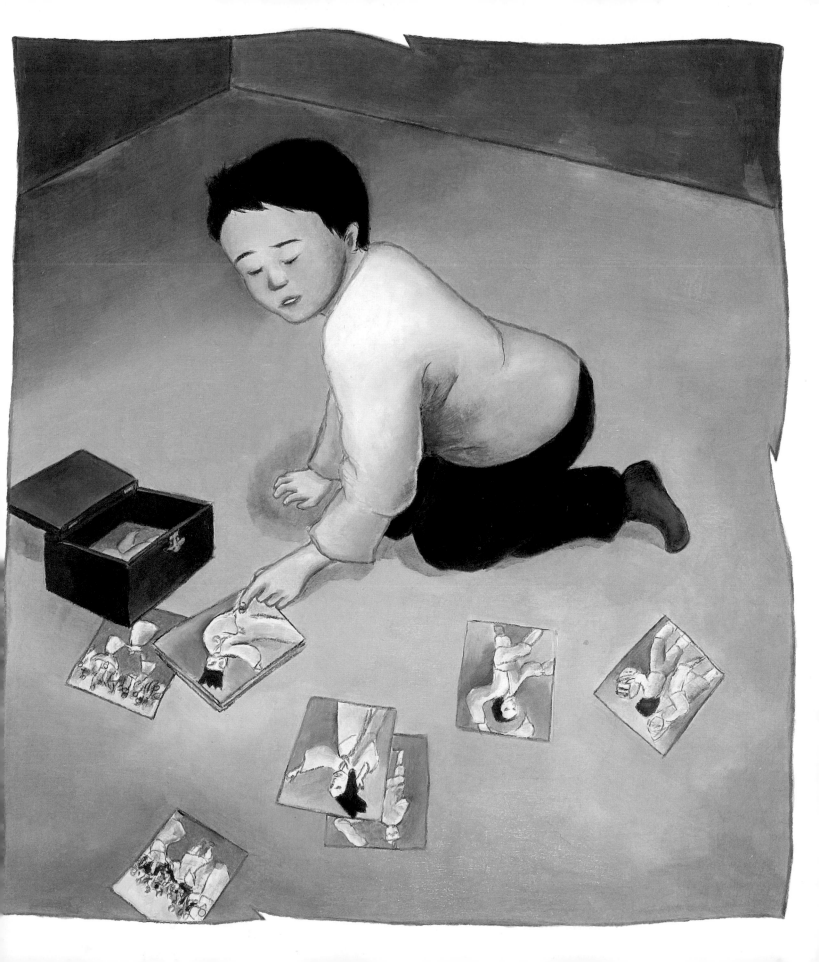

Kimin's curiosity grew. He looked at the other box, which was labeled *Tal*. What is *Tal*? he wondered. Cautiously he lifted the lid.

There, neatly folded, were traditional clothes like those worn by the dancers in Grandfather's photos. Beneath the costumes were the masks—some smiling, some frowning, some fierce. But none seemed very frightening to Kimin now. They were fun to look at, and he laughed at his nervousness.

Then he saw the face that had frightened him that scary night in Korea! He ran to find his mother.

"What does *Tal* mean?" he asked.

"Oh, did you see your grandfather's *tal*? *Tal* means 'mask' in Korean," she said.

Now it all made sense to Kimin. Grandfather had been wearing a mask that night.

At school the next day, everyone was talking about Halloween.

"Jimmy is going to be an alligator, and I'll be a witch," said Emma. "What are you going to be?"

"I'll be my grandpa," Kimin said.

"You mean you're just going to dress up like an old man?" someone asked.

"Yes," said Kimin.

"That won't be much fun. You'll be too slow to follow us for trick or treat." The kids laughed at him, but Kimin didn't mind.

"Going as an old man is not very scary," they teased, but Kimin knew better.

Kimin hurried home after school. Today was the day for trick-or-treating. Kimin knew that Halloween was also a time to honor the dead.

Kimin lifted the mask his grandfather had worn that scary night out of the box. He looked into its face and felt as if Grandfather was speaking to him. Then he put it on and tied the black cloth attached to its rim at the back of his head.

He looked in the mirror and saw his grandpa as a mask dancer. He moved around the room, dancing as his grandpa did in the photos.

Then he put on Grandfather's dance clothes. They were too big, but that didn't matter. His costume was complete.

Kimin called goodbye to his mother. "Come home before dark," she answered, and he slipped out of the house before she could see that he was wearing a family treasure.

When he got to the street, he heard whispers and footsteps behind him.

"What are you?" a voice asked.

"I'm a mask dancer," answered Kimin.

Children in disguises surrounded him. "Show us your dance," said an alligator.

Kimin started dancing. The children watched in awe.

"Do you want to trick-or-treat with us?" the tuna asked.

The mask dancer nodded.

So they went from house to house, singing their song:

"Trick or treat, smell my feet, give me something good to eat."

The mask dancer danced, the children circled around him,
and they filled their pockets with treats.

It had suddenly turned from dusk to dark. It was time to go home.

Kimin didn't know how it happened, but he tripped on the hem of his coat and fell, face first. His mask hit the ground with a thud.

Quickly he took off the mask. The nose was scratched, but he was okay. The mask had protected him.

"It's Kimin!" the children shouted. "He's the mask dancer!"

"Yes, but now I have to go," cried Kimin. He knew that his mother would be angry with him. And what would Grandfather have thought?

Kimin's mother was waiting for him.

"Is that what you wore? Grandfather's dance clothes and his mask?" She looked surprised and then pleased, until she saw the scratches on Grandfather's mask.

Kimin's heart was beating fast. His face was as pale as the mask as he started to tell his mother what had happened.

Then the doorbell rang.

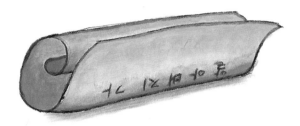

Kimin opened the door, and there stood all the children he had gone trick-or-treating with.

"Something fell out of your mask when you took it off," they said. The dragon handed Kimin a piece of folded paper.

Kimin opened it.

"What does it say?" the children asked.

"I don't know because it's written in Korean," said Kimin, handing the paper to his mother.

She looked at it, then translated it aloud:

Kimin,

Behind the mask my spirit remains. I want you to have it. Time will pass and the mask will get old, but I will be with you always.

—From Grandfather

"It's a letter from your grandpa!" the children exclaimed.

A smile lit up Kimin's face.

"Why don't you show your friends your grandfather's other *tal* and his photographs?" his mother said.

Kimin took the children to his room. They looked at the masks and the pictures, and soon everyone was dancing.

Later that night, Kimin and his mother hung Grandfather's masks on the wall above his bed.

"I am happy that you wanted to be your grandfather today," said his mother. "And don't worry about the mask. Grandpa would be happy that you found it."

In his heart, Kimin knew that was true.

AUTHOR'S NOTE

Talchum, or mask dance, is a traditional Korean folk dance. Masked dancers—traditionally peasants and farmers—enact dramas in song and dance, often criticizing and making fun of the ruling class. Characteristic and charming features of *Talchum* are its free and witty expression of emotions and the interaction between performers and audience. Toward the end of a play, the audience joins the dancers in a lively finale. *Talchum* performances are usually held outdoors.